Ant and Snail

Written by Paul Shipton
Illustrated by Jon Stuart

Collins

Ant and Snail had a run.

Ant was fit.
Ant was fast.

Snail was not fit.
Snail was not fast.

Ant did not wait for Snail.
He ran off fast.

Ant ran past the big rock.
He did not puff and
he did not pant.

Snail got to the big rock and
had a rest.

Ant ran past the grass.
He did not stop.

Ant hit a stick.
He fell in a pit.

Ant was stuck in the pit.

Snail got to the top
of the pit at last.

Snail put the stick in the pit.
Ant ran up it.

Ant and Snail sat on a rock and had a rest.

A map

rock

14

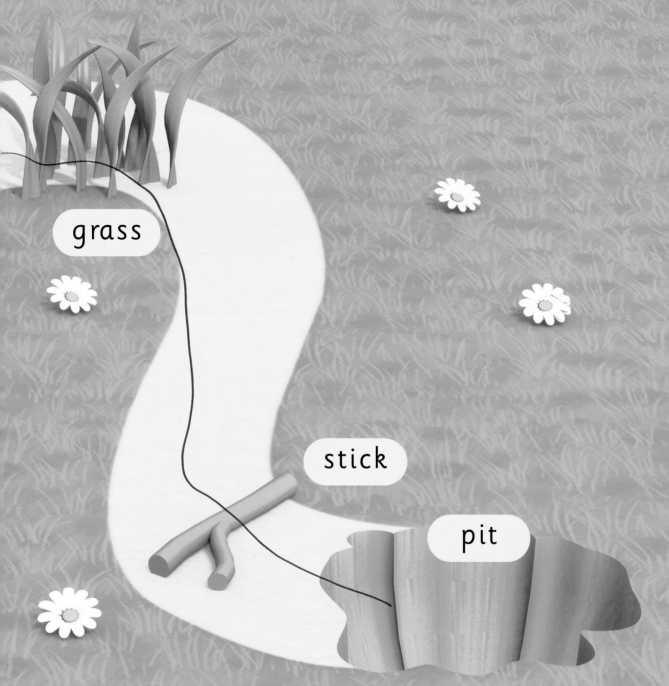

grass

stick

pit

15

❖ Ideas for reading ❖

Learning objectives: Hear and say sounds in words in the order in which they occur; Extend vocabulary, exploring the meanings and sounds of new words; Use their phonic knowledge to read simple regular words; Use talk to organise and sequence thinking, ideas, feelings, events; Attempt writing for different purposes.

Curriculum links: Creative development:

Explore colour, texture, shape, form and space in two and three dimensions.

Focus phonemes: n (run, not, ran, in), r (run, ran, rock, rest), f (fit, fast), ai (snail)

Other new phonemes: a, t, i, n , c, e, o, r, m, d, g, u, l, h, f, b

Fast words: was, the, to, he

Word count: 111

Getting started

- Write the words that include the focus phonemes *n*, *r*, *f* and *ai* on a small whiteboard and ask the children to fast-read them, blending through any words that they have difficulty with.

- Practise saying the *ai* phoneme together when blending *snail* and explain that when these two letters appear together they make a new, different sound.

- 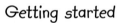 Write up the following words *ant, fast, snail, and* on the whiteboard. They all contain consonant clusters. Model how to blend the "s" and "n" in *snail* and encourage children to attempt the other words you have written up.

- Ask the children to fast-read the irregular fast words listed above in preparation for encountering them in the book.

- Read the blurb on the back cover together. Does it remind them of another story (the fable *The Hare and the Tortoise*)? *What do they think might happen?*

Reading and responding

- Give the children copies of the book to read independently. Move round the group to check that children are attempting to blend along the words that contain consonant clusters.